This book
was donated
to the
Lowell School
Library
by

ANDREA BAIER

2001

# LACROSSE

## THE NATIONAL GAME OF THE IROQUOIS

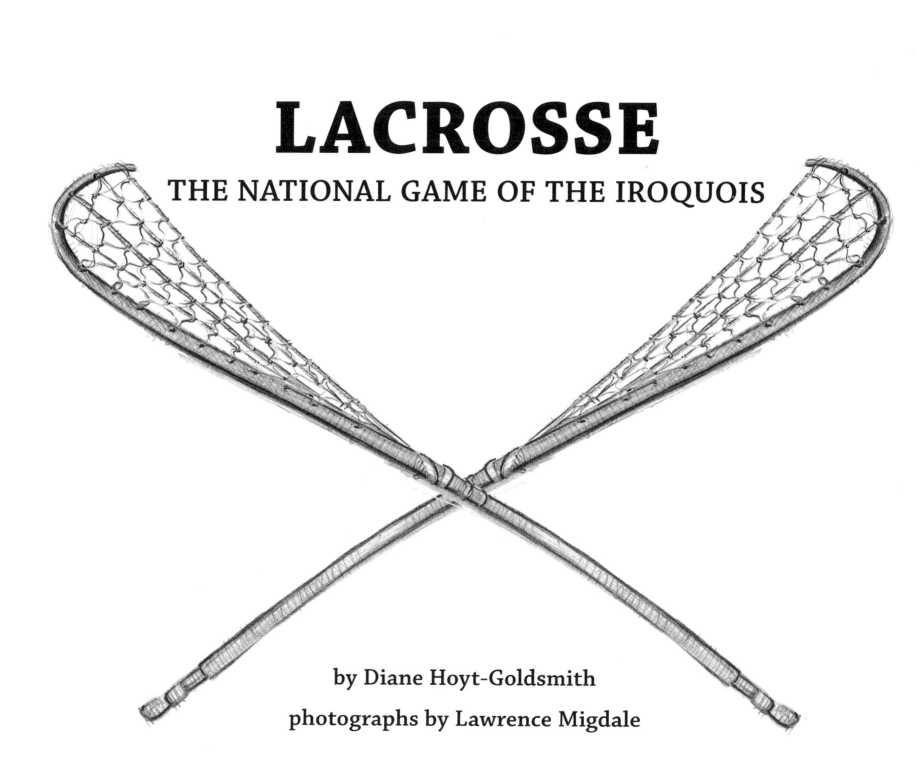

by Diane Hoyt-Goldsmith

photographs by Lawrence Migdale

Holiday House – New York

**Library of Congress Cataloging-in-Publication Data**

Hoyt-Goldsmith, Diane.

   Lacrosse: the national game of the Iroquois / by Diane Hoyt-Goldsmith;

photographs by Lawrence Migdale. — 1st ed.

      p.   cm.

  Includes index.

  Summary: Describes the sport of lacrosse, its origins, and connections to the Iroquois,

or Haudenosaunee, peoples.

  ISBN 0-8234-1360-8 (hardcover)

  1. Lacrosse—United States—Juvenile literature.  2. Iroquois Indians—United States—

Social life and customs—Juvenile literature.  [1.Lacrosse.  2. Iroquois Indians—Games.

3. Indians of North America—Games.]  I. Migdale, Lawrence, ill.  II Title.

GV989.H69  1998                                                                         97-37742

796.34'7—dc21                                                                        CIP

                                         AC

**Acknowledgments**

We would like to thank the entire Lyons family for all their help and cooperation in preparing this book. We are especially grateful to Monte for taking the time to teach us about lacrosse and for sharing his enthusiasm for the sport. Rex and Zina were generous with their time and hospitality, and Brook was a great help. We couldn't have done anything without Bev and her tireless planning and coordinating behind the scenes. Thanks to Oren Lyons for sharing the history of the game with us and for giving us his perspectives as a player, a coach, and a national leader of the Iroquois. Thanks to Lonnie Lyons and to Joe Cronin for all their support and cooperation.

    We were fortunate to spend a winter's day in the company of Alf Jacques, watching as he created fine wooden lacrosse sticks. We are grateful for the insights he shared with us.

    Thanks to Kevin Bucktooth, Monte's lacrosse coach, for helping us understand the rules of the game and to Chief Irving Powless for all his help.

    A special thanks goes to our friend Ed Burnam, a Mohawk and a lacrosse player, who inspired us to write this book and introduced us to the Lyons family.

    For more information about lacrosse, please contact US Lacrosse, Inc. and the Lacrosse Hall of Fame at 113 West University Parkway, Baltimore, Maryland  21210, 410.235.6882, or on the Internet at http://lacrosse.org.

Wearing the uniform of the Warriors, Monte gets ready to play a game in the Onondaga Territory. He also plays on the Camillus Middle School team called the Wildcats.

Thirteen-year-old Monte Lyons has been playing lacrosse for as long as he can remember. He first picked up a lacrosse stick at age three and played on a team when he was five. He has been involved in the sport ever since.

Monte, his brother Brook, and his parents are all American Indian citizens of the Onondaga Nation, one of the Six Nations of the Iroquois Confederacy.

The Onondaga Nation Territory is located south of Syracuse near Nedrow, New York.

At home, Monte and Brook enjoy learning about science on their computer.

In the wintertime, the boys look for solid ice in the stream near their grandmother's house. If they find it, they can play hockey.

Monte's Family Compound

Longhouse

Fairgrounds

Lacrosse Box

Making hot *skoons* from scratch is a traditional part of Monte and Brook's home life. Monte's grandmother lives next door to them and, although she doesn't play lacrosse herself, she has been driving her children and grandchildren to games for more than twenty years.

Monte and Brook find plenty of opportunities for off-road adventures in the Onondaga Territory.

Monte and Brook have spent many hours playing lacrosse with their friends in the box in the Onondaga Territory.

5

**(Left) Monte with his parents and his nine-year-old brother, Brook.**

**(Right) Monte and Brook keep their lacrosse trophies and awards in a room in their grandmother's house.**

Monte was born into a family that has been playing lacrosse for many generations. His father, Rex Lyons, played professionally for the Rochester Knighthawks. His grandfather, Oren Lyons, still plays lacrosse and is the chairman of the Iroquois Nationals team. He has traveled with the team to international competitions in England, Australia, and Japan. For Monte and his family, lacrosse is more than a game. It is a link to their ancestors and traditional culture.

# The Six Nations of the Iroquois

The Onondagas are one of the six nations of the Iroquois Confederacy. According to oral history, the union of the Seneca, Cayuga, Oneida, Mohawk, and Onondaga nations has been in existence since sometime between 1000–1200 A.D. The Tuscarora became the sixth nation. They left their original homeland in what is now North Carolina in about 1713 because of a devastating war with the colonists. They then moved north and were sponsored by the Oneidas, joining the confederacy in 1722.

French settlers in North America gave these people the name Iroquois. Their name for themselves is Haudenosaunee, which means "People of the Longhouse." Longhouses were their homes. Long and narrow, these had enough room for many related families to live under one roof. Although they shared a common roof to protect them from the rain and cold, each family had partitions for privacy and its own fire.

**The longhouse was the traditional dwelling of the Iroquois.**

The Iroquois Confederacy is an early example of a democratic government. The nations of the Iroquois thought of their confederacy as a great longhouse. Its Grand Council was created to maintain peace and goodwill between its members. Delegates met to discuss problems and find solutions. They made laws for the common good of all the people. Because the council decisions had to be unanimous, it sometimes took a long time for them to come to an agreement.

The Seneca in the far west are known as the Keepers of the Western Door because they kept out invaders from that direction. The Mohawk in the east are known as the Keepers of the Eastern Door. The Onondaga, in the center, are the Firekeepers. They host all the nations at the Grand Council. The symbolic longhouse stretched all across the land of the Iroquois to protect the people under one "roof," or government. Unlike the French and English settlers who came from lands ruled by kings, the Iroquois lived under their own laws and constitution. They were a free people. Respect for the individual was a guiding principle of their government, based on the Great Law of Peace, GU-YA-NA-SHA-NA-GO-NAH.

**MOHAWK**
**Keepers of the Eastern Door**

**ONEIDA**

**CAYUGA**

**SENECA**
**Keepers of the Western Door**

**ONONDAGA**
**Firekeepers**

**TUSCARORA**

**In the 1700s, the Iroquois of the Six Nations maintained their homes and territories throughout what is now New York State.**

When delegates from the thirteen original colonies met to draft a constitution for a new government, the success of the Iroquois Confederacy inspired them. The Constitution of the United States includes many of the same principles as the Iroquois Confederacy's Great Law. In 1987, the United States Senate passed a resolution recognizing the importance of the Haudenosaunee contributions to the Constitution.

At the time of first contact between the Europeans and the Iroquois, the Indians did not have a written language by which to record their history or stories. Instead, they had a rich oral tradition. Certain people in each tribe were chosen and trained to remember and recite the important events and stories of the tribe.

**Today there is a longhouse in the Onondaga Territory that was built in a contemporary style. It is still the place where delegates to the Grand Council from the Six Nations come to meet and make decisions for the nations.**

The Iroquois developed a visual aid to help them remember. They wove pictures and symbols out of tiny shell beads called wampum. These belts and strings of wampum became a way to pass along their history to future generations.

When the Iroquois met to make treaties with the Europeans, a gift of white wampum showed that the Iroquois meant what they said. Then, when an agreement was made, they made a wampum belt to symbolize what the agreement said. Finally, another gift of wampum sealed the treaty. In Iroquois communities, the national custodians at Onondaga kept the wampum belts safe. Wampum belts are as important to the Iroquois as the parchment document called the Declaration of Independence is to American citizens.

Today most wampum belts are being returned by collectors and museums. In 1988, the Iroquois Confederacy negotiated with New York State for the return of these treasures. Now there are several dozen important wampum belts and strings under the care of the people in the Onondaga Territory.

Monte's grandfather explains the significance of several wampum belts. The small one in the middle, the Two Row Wampum, commemorates a treaty with the Dutch. It symbolizes that both nations are traveling together down the "river of life," the white man in his boat and the Indian in his canoe. They don't come together, but they travel in peace and friendship as long as "the sun rises in the east and sets in the west, as long as the river runs downhill and the grass grows green." The large belt, the Washington Covenant belt of 1794, commemorates a treaty signed by President George Washington. It shows two figures in the center near the longhouse, surrounded by thirteen other figures, each representing one of the original colonies of the United States. The figure on the left represents President Washington, leader of the colonists, and the figure on the right is the Todadaho, leader of the Haudenosaunee.

# The Oldest Game

Long before Europeans came to North America, many American Indian tribes were playing a ball game similar to lacrosse. Known as GUH-CHEE-GWUH-AI by the Haudenosaunee, it was played with a rawhide ball and a stick. The stick had a net at the end that was used to throw and catch the ball.

The game was played on flat, grassy meadows. Sometimes players cleared and leveled land to make a better playing field. The playing fields were never the same size. They could be several hundred yards long or they could stretch for a mile or more. Sometimes, when the ball went into the woods, the game just continued among the trees.

In the early Indian games, there were no limits to the number of players who could join in. For some of the larger contests, teams of several hundred would compete. Size didn't matter as long as both teams had the same number of players. Some ball games lasted for many days.

The game was part of the Indians' religious beliefs. Whether Algonquin or Iroquois, Cherokee or Creek, Sioux or Santee, all believed that the Creator gave them the game for a special purpose. Often the Creator's game helped resolve conflicts between groups, families or clans, and nations. When it was impossible to settle a disagreement by discussion, both parties would agree to play a game of ball. The winner of the game would also win the dispute.

Since the beginning, and first and foremost, GUH-CHEE-GWUH-AI has always been a medicine game played for the well-being of players, other individuals, and nations. The Iroquois also play in bad times, to cure or prevent disease, or to lift the hearts of the people. For the Iroquois, GUH-CHEE-GWUH-AI is a way to communicate with the spirit world.

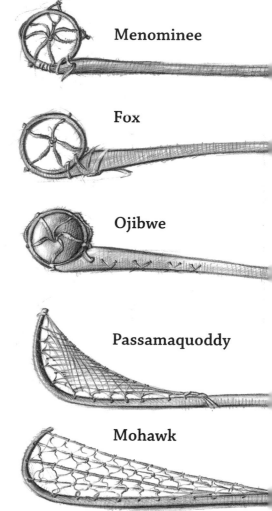

**Menominee**

**Fox**

**Ojibwe**

**Passamaquoddy**

**Mohawk**

**Different types of sticks were used by the various Native American groups in their ball games.**

Players prepared for the game physically, mentally, and spiritually. Often players called upon animal spirits to aid them during a game. Wearing a hawk's feather, a player prayed to be swift. A bear claw charm could make a player strong.

GUH-CHEE-GWUH-AI was played only by the men, but it was great entertainment for everyone in the community. Because the game made huge demands upon a player's strength and stamina, for some nations, it was also a way in which men stayed fit for hunting and combat.

In the 1830s, a painter named George Catlin traveled in North America making pictures of Indian life. After watching a Choctaw ball game, he painted this picture of the action.

13

# Lacrosse Becomes a Popular Sport

The first settlers who came from Europe were intrigued by the Indian ball games they saw. The French gave the game a new name — lacrosse. It was only a matter of time before the Iroquois taught the French and English to play.

A man from Montreal, Canada, named William George Beers became passionate about lacrosse. As a young boy, he had first seen the Mohawk teams compete at the nearby town of Caughnawaga. At school, Beers and his classmates got some lacrosse sticks and spent long hours practicing with them, trying to copy the skills of the Indian players they had seen.

**Monte's grandfather, Oren Lyons, is a Faithkeeper of the Iroquois Confederacy's Grand Council. He has been a lacrosse player since boyhood and played in college on Syracuse's 1957 undefeated team. In 1993, he was inducted into the Lacrosse Hall of Fame.**

Later in life Beers became a successful dentist, but he never lost his interest in lacrosse. In 1860, he published a short brochure on lacrosse in which he wrote down some "rules" of the game and described the positions of different players on the field. His book, *Laws of Lacrosse*, was published in 1869. Beers asked the government to make lacrosse the national sport of Canada, and on July 1, 1867, it did.

Soon lacrosse became popular in Canada, the United States, and many other parts of the world. Indian teams traveled to Europe to play before Queen Victoria in England and at the World's Fair in Paris. The English Lacrosse Association was formed in 1868 after people saw the Mohawk team play. By 1878, lacrosse had reached Australia and New Zealand.

Although American Indians created the game of lacrosse and had the most skilled players, for nearly a hundred years they were not allowed to compete in national or international games with white teams. In the 1880s, at the time lacrosse was becoming popular, many people were against professional sports — sports played for money. People like Beers and his friends had good jobs and could afford to play as a hobby. Indian players, however, came from different circumstances. Those who were lucky to have jobs received very little pay. When they charged admission to offset travel expenses, their teams were considered professional and therefore were not eligible to compete.

This did not change until 1987 when the Iroquois Nationals were accepted into the International Lacrosse Federation. They were invited to participate in the 1990 World Games in Perth, Australia. Monte's grandfather helped to organize the team for the trip and his father went as a player, scoring the most goals for the Iroquois Nationals team.

When the Iroquois Nationals team travels, they use a Iroquois passport. Provided by the Onondaga Nation Firekeepers of the Haudenosaunee, the passports are recognized by thirty-six countries in the world. Pictured on the cover is the great Tree of Peace, surrounded by clan emblems.

An Iroquois eagle dancer is the logo for the Iroquois Nationals lacrosse team.

# Field Lacrosse

The game of lacrosse has changed since the Indian ball games of the last century. Today, field lacrosse is a fast-moving contact sport between two teams of ten players. Each team moves the ball down the field using a lacrosse stick without ever touching the ball with their hands. They use the lacrosse stick to throw, catch, and carry it. Players try to shoot the ball into the net to score. The team with the most goals at the end of the game is the winner.

The playing field for today's lacrosse game is 110 yards long. The goals are set 80 yards apart. A regular football field can easily accommodate a lacrosse game.

One player on each team is a goalie and the rest of the team is divided into three attackmen, three midfielders, and three defensemen. The attackman, a position that Monte plays, stays near the opponent's goal and tries to score points for his team. The midfielders, also called "midis," cover the entire playing field, trying to set up plays so that the attackmen can score. They also help on defense. The defensemen stay near their own goal and try to keep the other team from scoring. The goalie's stick has a larger net at the end than a player's stick. The goalie tries to block shots on the goal with his stick or his body.

Today, lacrosse is played by both boys and girls, women and men. The women's game has a smaller playing field and some different rules.

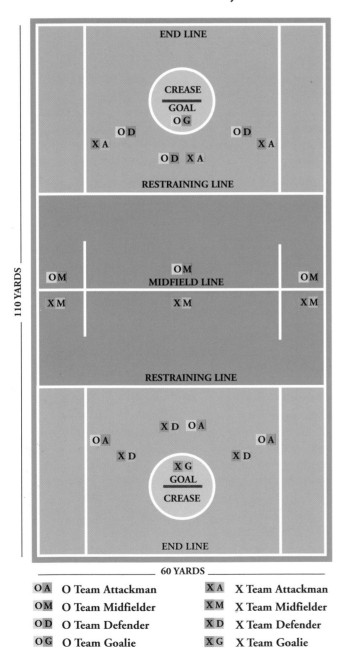

| OA | O Team Attackman | XA | X Team Attackman |
| OM | O Team Midfielder | XM | X Team Midfielder |
| OD | O Team Defender | XD | X Team Defender |
| OG | O Team Goalie | XG | X Team Goalie |

**Defenders use longer sticks than attackmen and midfielders. They use their crosses to check their opponents, trying to dislodge or steal the ball.**

Lacrosse is played with special equipment. The most important item is the lacrosse stick, also called the crosse. Made of either wood or a synthetic material such as plastic, the stick has a shaped pocket at one end that is used to scoop up, catch, and throw the ball. The ball is slightly smaller than a tennis ball and made of a hard, smooth rubber. Each player wears a helmet as well as a mouthpiece. Gloves and shoulder pads are mandatory for all the players except the goalie. Protective pads for arms, shoulders, and other parts of the body help prevent injuries.

The lacrosse season at Monte's school lasts from March until June. Monte practices two hours every afternoon and often plays two games each week. Twice a week all year round, Monte plays with the Onondaga youth lacrosse team called the Warriors.

**Monte's coach, Kevin "Bucky" Bucktooth, helps a player with his equipment.**

# Lacrosse Skills

**1. Face-off** — Lacrosse games begin with a face-off between two players of opposing teams. The ball is on the ground between Monte and Brook. When the umpire blows the whistle, each player tries to scoop up the ball.

**2. Cradling the Ball** — Using his arm and wrist, Monte maintains control of the ball in the net of his stick, even while running, turning, and stopping.

**3. Checking with the Stick** — In lacrosse, players may use the crosse to check an opponent. The stick can be used to strike the opponent's stick or gloved arm to knock the ball loose.

**4. Scooping the Ball** — Monte uses the stick to pick up the ball from the ground and gain control of it.

**5. Shooting** — With the crosse, Monte throws the ball toward the goal, trying to score a point.

**6. Catching and Passing** — With a quick wrist action and an overhead swing of his arms, Monte passes the ball to a teammate. Monte can also use the lacrosse stick to catch a ball in mid-flight.

## 1. Face-off

## 2. Cradling the Ball

## 3. Checking with the Stick

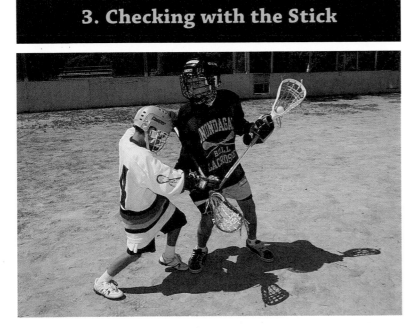

## 4. Scooping the Ball

## 5. Shooting

## 6. Catching and Passing

# Lacrosse - Traditional

Lacrosse is different from many other sports because all the ball handling is done with the lacrosse stick, or crosse. Used in place of the hands to throw, catch, and scoop the ball up from the ground, this stick can be made of wood and leather or of metal and plastic.

This photo of an Onondaga lacrosse team was taken in about 1900. Notice the old-style lacrosse sticks with the long, wide nets. Monte's great-great-uncles, Jessie Lyons and Ike Lyons, are members of this team.

# and Modern

Players on Native American teams often prefer to use the traditional wooden lacrosse stick. These are still made by hand by craftsmen in the Onondaga Territory.

Monte's team gathers for a portrait. Monte is standing right in front of the coach, Kevin Bucktooth. All the boys on the team are from the Onondaga Territory.

# Making a Traditional Lacrosse Stick

In the Onondaga Territory, Alf Jacques makes lacrosse sticks in the old way by hand.

In the wintertime, when the sap stops running in the trees, it is time to begin. First of all, Alf goes into the woods to find a smooth-bark hickory tree. He cuts it down and brings it back to his workshop.

Alf uses only the first eight feet of the tree. Here the wood grain is straight and clear of knots and limbs. Using a club and an ax, Alf splits the log into thin planks.

Next, Alf collects rainwater and heats it to make steam. He puts the planks into a steamer for several minutes until the hot, moist air has softened the wood enough so that he can bend it.

Alf puts the top of each piece of wood into a vise and bends it to form the head of the lacrosse stick. He ties a piece of wire around it to hold the shape as it dries.

Alf learned to make lacrosse sticks when he was a teenager. He wanted to play lacrosse with his friends, but he didn't have the money to buy a stick. His father, who was a carpenter, said to Alf, "Let's try to make a stick ourselves."

Together Alf and his father cut a tree down and started to make sticks. The first six broke in the process. By trial and error, they worked out the best way to make them. They invented or adapted tools for the job.

Alf and his father soon had a business making lacrosse sticks for other people. One year, they made 11,000 sticks. Alf played with the first stick he finished for ten years until he broke it in a game.

After the sticks are shaped, it takes eight to ten months for them to dry. Alf carves them with a special tool called a drawknife. He thinks that a wooden stick can help a player improve his game. Alf says that carving the crook is what puts "the magic" into a stick.

Monte's father prefers to play with a wooden stick.
"A wooden stick is made from the living wood of a tree," he says.
"When we play with a wooden stick, we are closer to nature,
to the Creator, and to the spiritual side of this game."

Today, most players use factory-made lacrosse sticks. Many players, however, prefer a handmade stick. No two are exactly alike. They are strong and light and have a flexibility that plastic sticks do not.

For a traditional lacrosse game, handmade wooden sticks are always used. For this reason, people like Alf Jacques are important to the Iroquois. They help to keep the lacrosse traditions alive.

Although Monte plays with both kinds of sticks, he prefers the wooden ones too. He has learned how to lace the nets for his sticks. Sometimes he earns extra spending money by lacing nets for other players.

# Box Lacrosse

In the 1930s, a new version of lacrosse became popular. Often played indoors on ice rinks during hockey's off-season, box lacrosse is becoming more popular than field lacrosse on the East Coast and in Canada. Box lacrosse is played with six players on a team rather than ten. The positions are goalie, center, two forwards, and two defense-men. As in ice hockey, entire lines of players can switch on and off the playing field, depending on whether the team is on offense or defense. Box lacrosse is a rougher game, with lots of body and stick checking. This form of the game sets a grueling pace and requires athletes who are very fit.

**An outdoor game of box lacrosse between two teams in the Onondaga Territory brings out a fierce competition between players.**

**A shot on goal brings the defensemen in to help the goalie.**

A number of cities have professional box lacrosse teams. For two seasons, Monte's father was a forward for the Rochester Knighthawks, one of six professional teams playing in the Northeast. The other teams are the Buffalo Bandits, New York Saints, Boston Turbos, Philadelphia Wings, and Baltimore Thunder.

Box lacrosse is also very popular among the Iroquois in the territories. Monte plays center for his box lacrosse team. In the Onondaga Territory, the people have constructed a box where players in each age group compete.

# Lacrosse in the Onondaga Territory

Lacrosse in the Onondaga Territory is for everyone. Young people watch their fathers and grandfathers, brothers and uncles playing the game. They handle sticks from a young age. Kids grow up seeing lacrosse played both for fun and for ceremonial reasons. They learn about its long history with the Iroquois. Lacrosse is part of their way of life.

**Monte's team hosts an exhibition game against the Oneida team in the box built near the fairgrounds in the Onondaga Nation Territory.**

Each year at the end of the summer, the Onondaga hold a cultural fair and celebration. For three days, people are invited to come witness the dances, taste the foods, and hear the music of the Onondaga people. Special crafts such as handmade lacrosse sticks, corn husk dolls, and traditional clothing are sold. There are lots of activities as well, including a series of lacrosse games between the Onondaga and teams from other Iroquois nations.

**When Monte's family gets together for an afternoon barbecue, they usually end up playing a game of lacrosse.**

Through the years, lacrosse has become a sport that is enjoyed by players and fans all over the world. Even so, it has not lost its importance in the ceremonial life of the Haudenosaunee.

Today the People of the Longhouse have moved to many different parts of North America. There are now sixteen different territories in the United States and Canada. They are located in New York, Wisconsin, Oklahoma, Ontario, and Quebec. Some Iroquois, like the Onondaga, still live in the same place as their ancestors did. Other Iroquois have been forced over the years to leave their homelands. However, wherever the Haudenosaunee live, they are still playing the game of lacrosse. It unites them and makes them proud. It is a tradition that links them to their history. Monte and his family know that lacrosse is an important contribution to modern life, but it is also a treasured part of their American Indian heritage and a link to their culture, identity, and past.

# Glossary

**attackmen** Three players in the game of field lacrosse who try to score goals.

**box lacrosse** A version of lacrosse played within an enclosed wooden structure, rink, or box, located outdoors or indoors.

**Cayuga** (ky-OOH-gah) One of the Six Nations of the Iroquois Confederacy.

**checking** Hitting the gloved arm of a player with the lacrosse stick to dislodge the ball, or blocking a player with the body.

**cradling** Carrying a ball in the net of a lacrosse stick.

**crease** In field lacrosse, a circular area 18 feet in diameter that surrounds the goal. Attackmen cannot enter the crease around the goal but they may reach in with their sticks to scoop up a loose ball.

**crosse** A short term for lacrosse stick.

**defensemen** Three players in the game of field lacrosse whose jobs are to prevent the other team from scoring.

**drawknife** A carving tool craftsmen use to shape the curve at the top of the lacrosse stick.

**face-off** When two players of the opposing teams try to put the ball in play at the beginning of a game or period.

**field lacrosse** A version of lacrosse played outdoors on a flat, open field.

**goalie** A player in lacrosse who defends the goal. Each team has one goalie.

**GUH-CHEE-GWUH-AI** A Haudenosaunee name for the ancient Indian ball game from which the modern game of lacrosse was adapted.

**GU-YA-NA-SHA-NA-GO-NAH** A Haudenosaunee term for the Great Law of Peace upon which the government of the Six Nations of the Iroquois is based.

**Haudenosaunee** (hoh-dee-noh-SHO-nee) A term that means "people of the longhouse" and the name that the Iroquois gave themselves.

**Iroquois Confederacy** (EER-oh-qwoy) The Six Nations of the Iroquois, made up of the Seneca, Cayuga, Onondaga, Oneida, Tuscarora, and Mohawk tribes.

**longhouse** A long, narrow building large enough to house several related families and the traditional dwelling of the Iroquois.

**Mohawk** (MOH-hawk) One of the Six Nations of the Iroquois Confederacy, known as Keepers of the Eastern Door.

**Oneida** (oh-NY-dah) One of the Six Nations of the Iroquois Confederacy.

**Onondaga** (AH-non-DAH-gah) One of the Six Nations of the Iroquois Confederacy, known as the Firekeepers.

**Seneca** (SEH-neh-kah) One of the Six Nations of the Iroquois Confederacy, known as Keepers of the Western Door.

**scooping** Picking up the ball with a lacrosse stick.

**shooting** Throwing the ball toward the goal with a lacrosse stick.

*skoons* A slang term in the Onondaga Territory for homemade fry bread.

**Todadaho** The name for the leader of the Iroquois people.

**territory** The land occupied by the people of a sovereign nation.

**Tuscarora** (TUS-cah-ROAR-ah) The last group to join the Six Nations of the Iroquois Confederacy.

**wampum** Tiny beads made from seashells and woven together to form strings or belts. The strings and belts are artifacts the Iroquois use to pass along their history and stories from one generation to the next.

## The Hiawatha Wampum

The Hiawatha Wampum symbolizes the union between the five original nations of the Haudenosaunee as well as the birth of democracy in North America. In about 1000 AD, the People of the Longhouse formed a constitutional government based on the principles of Peace, Equity, Justice, Health, and Power.

The design on the wampum represents the Longhouse. Starting from left to right, the first square represents the Mohawk Nation, Elder Brother and Keeper of the Eastern Door; the next square represents the Oneida Nation and Younger Brother; the central symbol is the Tree of Peace depicting the Onondaga Nation, Elder Brother and Firekeeper of the union. To the West, the next square represents the Cayuga Nation and Younger Brother; the last square represents the Seneca Nation, Elder Brother and Keeper of the Western Door. The belt is like a map of the original five nations of the Iroquois Confederacy.

The tabs extending on each side of the design show that other nations could follow the white roots of the Tree of Peace to its source and petition the Grand Council for admission to the confederacy. The Tuscarora Nation did just that in 1713 and by 1722 had become the sixth member nation of the Haudenosaunee.

To celebrate their national heritage and commemorate the recent return of the Hiawatha Wampum to the Haudenosaunee by the New York State Museum, the Haudenosaunee flag was created using the Hiawatha Belt as an inspiration. The design on the flag is an exact replica of the Hiawatha Belt. It was flown for the first time in 1990 at the International Lacrosse Federation World Games in Perth, Australia. The flag was flown with Six Eagle Feathers to symbolize the addition of the Tuscarora Nation to the Haudenosaunee.

## Index